THE NEW BUG

SCHOOL FOR BUGS

by Elizabeth Bennett
Illustrated by Jeffrey Scherer

SCHOLASTIC INC.

New York   Toronto   London   Auckland   Sydney
Mexico City   New Delhi   Hong Kong   Buenos Aires

To my boys, Bennett and Jeremy
— E.B.

For Frank, my best friend since 1966
— J.S.

ISBN 0-439-46641-5

Text copyright © 2003 by Elizabeth Bennett.
Illustrations copyright © 2003 by Jeffrey Scherer.
All rights reserved. Published by Scholastic Inc.
SCHOLASTIC, THE BUG BUNCH, and associated logos are trademarks and/or registered trademarks of Scholastic Inc.

12 11 10 9 8 7 6 5 4 3 2 1   3 4 5 6 7 8/0
Printed in the U.S.A. • First printing, March 2003 • Book design by Mark Freiman

CONTENTS

CHAPTER ONE
SCHOOL BELL

The school bell rang.

Buzz, Lady, and Spy are getting

ready to go home.

Stretch walks up

to join them.

"Has anyone seen

Stinky?" he asks.

"No," answers Spy.

STRETCH

LADY

STINKY

5

"I didn't even see him at lunch,"
says Buzz.

"Come on, guys," says Stretch. "Stinky
would never miss lunch."

"I saw him there," adds Lady. "But he
wasn't sitting at our table."

"Where was he?" asks Stretch.

CHAPTER TWO
THE NEW BUG

Stinky had lunch with
the new bug at school.

And Stinky is with the new bug now.

The new bug's name is Spike.

He just moved to town.

Spike is in Stinky's class.

Stinky has been spending more and more time with Spike.

And less and less time with the Bug Bunch.

"I miss Stinky," sighs Stretch.

CHAPTER THREE
SKATEBOARDS

Now the Bug Bunch are walking

home from school.

Two bugs are coming up behind

them on skateboards.

It is Stinky and Spike.

"Hey, Stinky!" calls Stretch.

"How's the air up there?" cries Spike.

"See you later, Beanpole!"

shouts Stinky.

Off they go on their skateboards.

Stretch hangs his head down.

He feels very small.

CHAPTER FOUR
SHOP TALK

The Bug Bunch stop to get ice cream.

Stinky and Spike are already there.

They are both eating ice-cream cones.

Stinky is having his favorite flavor—

a triple scoop of sardine caramel swirl.

Yuck!

Buzz wants a honey vanilla cone.

"Watch out, Stinky," says Spike loudly.

"Don't get too close to that bee,

he might sting you."

Lady wants a chocolate chip cone.

"What are you ordering, Freckle Shell?"

calls Stinky.

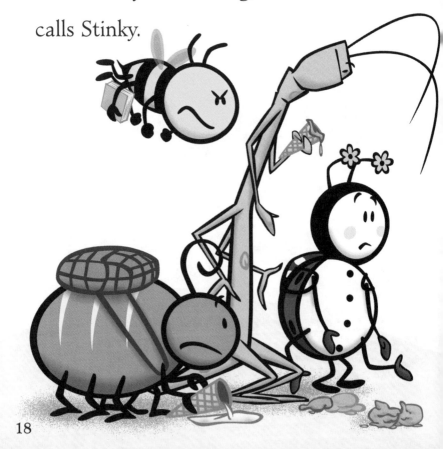

Spike and Stinky laugh as they leave the shop.

Buzz and Lady decide not to get any ice cream.

They are not hungry anymore.

CHAPTER FIVE
OLD FRIEND

The Bug Bunch walk home.

They are very quiet.

Stretch is the first to talk.

"I miss Stinky," he says.

"But we just saw Stinky," says Spy.

"No, I mean I miss the *old* Stinky,"

answers Stretch.

"I know what you mean,"

adds Lady.

"I get it," says Buzz. "Stinky wants that new bug to like him."

"So, he is acting mean just like Spike," says Stretch.

CHAPTER SIX
WELCOME BACK

Whaaa! Whaaa!

Someone is crying.

It is Stinky.

Stretch runs over to him.

"What's wrong? Are you hurt?"
asks Stretch.
"Spike called me Skunk Breath,"
says Stinky. "I thought
he was my friend."

"Friends don't call each other names,"
adds Lady.

"I called you names," says Stinky.

"We know," says Buzz.

"I just wanted Spike to like me," explains Stinky.

"We know," says Buzz.

"Spike is really mean," adds Stinky.

"We know," says Buzz.

"I'm really sorry," says Stinky.

"We know," says Buzz.

"Welcome back, Stinky!"

the Bug Bunch cheer.

THE END

Bug Bunch Fun Fact!

A rhinoceros beetle is a kind of horned beetle. It can support up to 850 times its own weight on its back. That would be the same as a man carrying 76 family-size cars around on his back.